01

We had to travel 4 hours by train and I would have loved to spend Christmas with my friends and especially with my girlfriend. We've been together for three weeks and she's our first real friend. So far I've had a few but not too much had gone with them.

It's different with Sabine, we quickly expressed our wishes and they were almost identical and so it annoys me all the more that we are still participating in this family celebration. My father died in an accident at work four years ago and we spend a few weeks vacation with my grandparents every year. So today was such a really bad day that you already know that when you get up. Just crap torn pants while putting them on. Pulling the suitcase into the taxi handle ripped off. The taxi driver smelled like thirteen camels. And the station is totally overcrowded. 12 minutes left until our train arrives. I watch some people on our platform. I think to myself when I see a mother and daughter, they're definitely sitting in the compartment with us. The mother gives the impression of being a teacher at a Catholic boarding school.

The old one is just nagging, not tapping her feet. Put your feet together. Our train comes in with the suitcases,

compartments look for suitcases up in the storage grids. I'm sitting, the door opens and these people, as I had feared, come in.

My mother, of course, Bernd, please help the young women. I also packed up my suitcase and in a bad mood I sat down again. Both mothers immediately blablabla Christmas with the parents-in-law bla bla always nice bla bla I have to choke. The daughter across from me and keeps nudging me with her shoe.

I was just about to formulate a few appropriate words, look at me with a look that would have even made the Pope sweat. She smiles and looks at her mother. But they are so busy with family stories that they don't notice anything. A few stations further on, she asks her mother if she can get some money for a soda. Of course, directly you don't go there alone, you have to wait until she goes with you and so on. My mother directly Bernd can accompany her daughter and get something to drink.

So now the measure is full but the little one immediately high and takes me by the hand. Now I can also play babysitter. As soon as we closed the door, she tells me that her mother is getting on her nerves and that she is glad when they are finally here. We get something in the food wagon and stroll through the compartments until she pulls me into an empty compartment. She hangs it around my neck and kisses me. At first I just thought of getting out of here, but then her wet tongue was busy with mine and I thought that it might be a good way to pass the time.

After a few short breaks, she grabbed my pants and asked me if I wanted to fuck her. I stopped spitting. The beast on the outside so prudish and under the clothes such a little witch. Yes, of course, but we should see our mothers again beforehand. In our compartment still blah blah my husband and my husband blah blah. Andrea that's her name, doesn't she ask stupidly if we can't walk around the train a little bit because of stretching our legs and stuff like that. But only if Bernd goes with you. I made a pissed face of course but then after her.

At the end of the wagon we go into the disabled toilet. Andrea immediately took off her jacket and kissed me. At the same time she opens her skirt and my pants. I was then told I could do something and not just stand there stupidly. Our tongues no longer parted and our clothes were placed neatly on the sink by her. Now I could see her breasts that didn't need to be hidden. Beautifully round and firm with large dark areolas and large nipples.

She had styled her pussy a bit and the lust was already dripping out of her. She massaged my rod and said that she shouldn't inject herself because it could be seen in her underwear. If it came to me I should let her know and she would then suck him dry. That was an announcement and she had pushed the thing in below. She was so horny that she came after a few short thrusts and I had to hold her tight. I turned her over and she put one leg over the handrails.

It was even better from behind, her pussy was hot and slippery. She probably hadn't held out her butt that often because she was watching exactly what I was doing. I grabbed her hips with both hands and pumped my spear harder and harder into her. She came a second time and I was also beginning to have an orgasm. She groaned loudly and I had to think of her mother if she could hear it. Her knees went weak and I slowed my pace. She turned around and kissed me while massaging my spear nicely. "Can't you?" she asked. Of course I can but I told her my thoughts and we had to laugh heartily. She went down on me and licked my penis first gently and then harder.

"You have a nice penis, so nice and even and thick." "Thanks for the compliment," I replied. A few times she almost swallowed him whole and had to choke. "It's too big, I can't get it all the way in". I had an idea. To the right and left of the toilet were handrails on which I placed her legs and her pussy was now at a comfortable height. I knelt in front of her and looked Her cleft a little more precisely.The labia are thick and red, the smaller ones only hinted at and small on the inside.The clitoris at the upper end is also swollen and dark red.

Her lust dripped into the toilet bowl and I licked her outer lips up to the clitoris. I lingered on him and gently sucked on him. Her lust rose immeasurably. She could barely stand on the bars and said, "Come on, fuck me again." I complied immediately and pushed my penis all the way into her hole. She was out of her mind and I had to hold her so she wouldn't pee the toilet falls. It's really fun to watch her go off one after the other. Now I was about to have an orgasm too. I pulled out my penis and she sat on the toilet bowl and sucked it and massaged it with her hands at the same time the shaft.

An enormous gush shot out of me that she couldn't quite absorb and so my sperm ran down the corners of her mouth. A few drops fell on her breasts, leaving wet tracks on her skin. My outpouring wasn't quite over when I heard her start peeing. I must have looked a little stupid because she grinned at me and without letting my slowly shrinking mouth out of her mouth she said "Since I'm here. And whenever I've been fucked like that, I have to pee anyway."

After it was finished, I thought to myself what you can do, I can do it for a long time and let it run. I aimed right between her legs and she scratched my testicles. I didn't come to shake it off, she did it for me. We freshened up a bit and put on our clothes. She stuffed another ball of toilet paper in her panties "There's still some dripping." She really was a naturally horny little beast. Now in her gray suit she looked like nothing could come to her mind. We slowly walked to ours compartment not without pinching my butt a few more times.In front of the compartment she kissed me again quickly and indicated silence with her finger.

Our mothers were still blah blah and then we're at the beach blah blah. Why can women without knowing each other actually talk to each other for hours without having a topic. I made myself a little more comfortable and fell asleep a little. The background noise was so nice and sleepy. I woke up when the railway officials came and checked the tickets again. Andrea threw me one of her eyes again and asked if we could not walk a little through the train again. I stretched and said "Why not?" My mother grinned at me and warned us not to long, we have to get off in half an hour. Andrea's mother agreed with the statement "Yes, we too". Of course, Andrea only had one thing in mind, she wanted to FUCK a little more quickly.

She directed me straight to the handicapped toilet and immediately got to work on my pants. I threw my jacket and shirt straight onto the sink and opened Andrea's blouse. I didn't come to undress because she almost had my hard-on stuck in her throat and was sucking on it. "Slow down or the shot will go off too soon," I admonished her. After she was satisfied with her work and he was standing like one, she quickly undressed and put her legs over the handrails. "Come here and put it in. This was the best fuck I've had so far and I absolutely have to have it again". She was again or still so horny that it dripped out of her. It was a breathtaking sight as her pussy was there so open in front of me and I sucked on her small nipple.

She was extremely sensitive and reacted to every touch. "Now fuck me fuck me fuck me" she yelled at me. Her unbridled lust only made me hesitate a little more. I gently ran a finger over her clit, which immediately stood up and peeked out of the skin fold. Andrea got furious and tried to bite me I pressed her against the wall with one hand and licked down at her pussy Her juice tasted amazing and her clit even more sensitive She couldn't suppress her orgasm it came like a hurricane over her and a gush escaped from her pussy and dripped back into the toilet bowl.

When she was just beginning to recover, I pushed my cock into her pussy and just as quickly she was up to speed again. I pumped into the small one with force and it rose up at the last moment, I thought about not injecting into her and pulled him out. Almost too late the first shot was fired already there he was just millimeters away from her clitoris and the beam was pattering directly at him. The second squirted over her stomach and breasts up to her neck. The rest I placed on her stomach and it ran down her and also dripped into the toilet bowl. She sat down and licked my spear. "You're supposed to cum in my mouth, I like that. Now the good stuff is wasted". Let someone understand this little beast. We got ready and went back to the compartment.

We sat down and Andrea looked at me and spread her legs a bit so I could see her panties. She couldn't help but then we had to get out and I politely said goodbye. Grandpa and grandma were already waiting for us at the train station. After a brief greeting, we went to the car and drove to my grandparents' farm. On the way they said that there might be some space problems because all their children and many of their grandchildren were already there. After I thought on the train that this lousy day would be over, I was now taught better. I should definitely sleep in a room with my twin cousins, but I can't survive that.

Last year they almost drove me crazy. We drove out of the city into the country and it had already snowed here. My thoughts were now with Andrea as I polish her pussy again and she drips so nicely. Of course, my little one makes itself felt and my mother nudges me, looks at my trousers and says "It wasn't Bernd". My head wanted to burst immediately and I only got a "pump" out and had no idea what they had talked about. We arrived at the farm and Aunt Rosi and Aunt Katrin greeted us. At least one ray of hope Rosi is the best aunt you can imagine. She is my father's youngest sister and is always fond of us young people.

We've been to her house a lot and I really like her. She has no children but wears men like pants. Aunt Katrin is also fine if it weren't for her twins. Kisses were greeted here and there and then we went inside. I put our suitcases down in the hallway and Katrin said to my mother, "Erika, you can sleep with me." My mother looked at me and my pulse rose because now all I could do was "The Twins". "Then Bernd can sleep with me" called Rosi from behind. My mother looked at me and then at Rosi. Her gaze darkened and when she was about to say something Rosi said "Or do you want to lock him up with the twins". I say yes, it's great. "That wouldn't bother them either," Katrin replied.

She has a great figure and is always dressed chic without exception. She usually wears a skirt and matching jacket. A sweater or blouse underneath and always high heels. No wonder that the men in front of her door are flat on their feet. The others always whisper when she has a new one, but she doesn't care. We had the small guest bedroom down the hall. On the balcony you could almost walk around the whole house. From here you have a good view over the courtyard to the horse stables.

I put my suitcase on the bed and Rosi said "Come here, I'll help you unpack quickly". She took the shirts and sweaters and opened the closet. Some of her things were already in there. I grabbed my socks and underpants and opened the drawer at the dresser. Oops, she was already wearing her underwear and there was a rubber cock on top. I had never seen one in person and couldn't take my eyes off it. Rosi noticed it and came over to me. "Well, what are you doing here you belong somewhere else" it said and took it out of the drawer and brought it to the bedside table. I was still standing there stupidly and she said, "You know what that is, don't you? You can imagine what women do with it. Have you ever tried one with your girlfriend?"

"It's not coming yet, it's not that bad." After my things were stowed away, we talked a little longer and she noticed that I didn't have any pajamas and wanted to know if I slept naked. Yes, of course, at home and actually I wanted to have packed one. "That's not bad from me, you can sleep naked, I often do that too." she waved me off. "Let's go downstairs, I'm sure there will be food soon".

In the kitchen, Grandma was just about to put everything on the table. When she saw me she said to me "Go and get Grandpa he's in the stable". Good idea I wanted to go into the stable anyway to check on the horses. Here everything was the same as before the whole area is covered with straw and each Horse has its own box. In the back area, familiar noises came to my ear. I quietly walked on and in an empty box my aunt Gerda was just being taken from behind by the stableman Jakob. I looked at it for a while and the idea came to me photographing it, I always had my little camera with me and I took some nice snapshots.

First on all fours from behind then missionary and cum over the big tits.

Gerda is the black sheep of the family, if I may say so. She has been married four times and the fifth is coming soon. Her five children are from just as many fathers. The two oldest, Rolf and Sylvia, already live alone and the third, Jeremias, is a Negro baby that she brought with her from a holiday in Africa. There was something going on when a dark-skinned child was born in the hospital. Her then husband moved out immediately and got a divorce. And then there are the two youngest, Sabine and Sandra. But now look for Grandpa, he must be in the other barn with the cows. When I found him he hugged me like an old buddy and we strolled across the yard together. He is curious and asks me about my girlfriend and the school. Then whether Mama doesn't slowly have a boyfriend again. We chat a little more like we always do, then grandma comes and hisses at us that the food is getting cold and everyone is already waiting. We hurry and go to the dining room.

Everyone is already at the table and I see my two cousins now. But they've changed a lot since last year. In their favor, of course. They are really pretty and have also matured, no wonder Aunt Katrin didn't want me to sleep with them. Of course, the meal didn't go without a few jokes about Gerda's new friend, who might also come along. Uncle Klaus is a military officer with no idea what exactly I'm glad he's on duty and won't come until after Christmas, because he's always trying to recruit me. Tiredness breaks out and I yawn in my cousins' faces. They immediately make fun of me because she wants to eat us and stuff like that.

If they bother me, I'll lock them up with the cows this year. After the meal I separate myself and walk around a bit to take a few photos. It's been my great passion for two years and I've already made some good pictures that have been shown in exhibitions. It's getting too dark and I decide to go back not without pressing the shutter button a few more times.

There is already a Christmas spirit in the house and Grandma sings all sorts of songs at once. The women are busy clearing the living room so that the Christmas tree can be picked up tomorrow. Dinner and the subsequent small drink come to an end without any further special events. Rosi then asks me if we're going to bed and gets the mean look from my mother again. It's quite late and I agree not without having another drink with my grandpa. Now I had four, that's enough the night belongs to me.

In the room, Rosi immediately opens her skirt and lets it fall elegantly onto a chair. It's not just the alcohol that strikes me now, but the sight of those long legs in stockings that are held up with suspenders and panties that don't deserve the word. She hangs her sweater over the back of the chair and notices how I look at her. "I think you've seen it all before. If it still bothers you, I'll go into the bathroom and change there," she said and wanted to leave the room. "No, it's just because I haven't seen these things so beautifully wrapped," I answered quickly and quickly got rid of mine Things. This little strip number didn't quite go by without me. My penis was half erect and wasn't hanging all the way down. "But you're also quite well endowed" Rosi said and pointed to my privates. Now he stood up a bit more and my head was pounding and threatened to explode. She took off her last clothes and slipped into a baby doll.

I had already made myself comfortable in bed and actually wanted to sleep quickly, but Rosi asked me about my girlfriend and the trip here. I told her about Andrea and she told her about her friend Jasmin with whom she had experienced a lot. It happened to her for the first time that she saw that a woman can secrete so much fluid. I was aware that Rosi is not a wallflower, but I would not have expected her to have a lesbian relationship. We talked for a while and then fell asleep.

I woke up and had to pee. No clock no light the bathroom was just opposite our room. Since I was facing the door, it was easy to get to the hallway with no light. I quietly closed the door behind me and was about to go to the bathroom when I heard a supposed noise. My voyeuristic inclination was awakened and I went after the sounds. The sounds came from the other end of the house, there was my grandparents' bedroom and Gerda's bedroom with her children.

I couldn't imagine who made these. I slipped silently around the corner and saw my two cousins in the dim light. They stood close together in front of my grandparents' door, one hand each under their nightgown. The door wasn't completely closed and the noise was clearly coming from there. I slowly approached them from behind and watched them both very closely. They were excited and jerked their pussy. "What are you doing!" I said under my breath and turned her shoulders. As if struck by lightning, their bodies froze and they couldn't even breathe anymore. Her gaze fell on me and at that moment I realized I was naked .

I threatened with my index finger and said, "You go straight to your room and wait until I come to you." They passed me like a storm and disappeared into the room. However, I couldn't resist a look through the crack in the door. Grandma just had a hard-on in her mouth and was sucking like a possessed woman. I changed my perspective and realized that someone else was banging her. Now I was a bit shocked my grandma with two men. With grandpa, of course, you could imagine that but who was the other.I waited a few minutes and they switched positions.Grandpa had just pleasured her and was now underneath her.She took his big cock in her can and started riding him.The other now came up to her from behind and tried to stick his no less big ass in her ass, which was also successful.

More minutes passed and grandma had come a few times because the man behind her squirted his cream all over her buttocks. Then he lay down next to the two and I almost popped my eyes out of my head. It was Jacob the stable boy. Now my breath caught and it took me a few seconds to catch myself. My full bladder actually brought me back to reality. I relieved myself and went to my cousins' room.

"I'll tell your mother about it in the morning and see what she thinks of it," I said, pretending to leave the room again. As if with one voice, they tried to persuade me to find another solution think about it until breakfast and then let you know". I went to my room and immediately fell asleep contentedly.

02

I slowly returned to reality from the dream world and felt something soft and warm in my right hand. The sun was just trying to peek over the first mountains and bathed our room in a purple robe. Suddenly I became aware of what I was holding in my hand. It was my aunt's chest and even worse my morning wood had found its way between my thighs. I was startled and wanted to pull away a little but her hand was on mine and pressed her tightly to her.

She had noticed my attempt to escape and murmured, "You don't want to leave me like that, do you?" I felt completely different and my penis liked it very much because it made itself as big as it could go do you want ..." my brain cells weren't all there yet and so I stammered something incomprehensible.

She turned and gently stroked my face and looked deep into my eyes. "It's nothing new for you to lie in bed with a woman and cuddle a little." Nothing new, no, but with my aunt. "But you're my aunt and that's not possible," I replied. She rolled her eyes and said, "You still haven't been told that your father isn't your biological father, right? He married your mother when she was already pregnant with you and at first everyone thought you were from him. Calculate your birthday and your parents' wedding, then you'll see that it's pretty close and I asked my brother about it and he then told me everything".

Now I was a bit shocked. They should have told me something like that a long time ago. I was snapped out of my thoughts by a knock on the door. Rosi called in. My cousins Sarah and Judith carefully put their heads in and looked at us. I had totally forgotten about that. "Come in," I said, waving my hand. Embarrassed and with bowed heads, they stood in front of our bed. Rosi looked at me questioningly. "So you two, how did you imagine that?"

Now they looked at each other and blushed and even more embarrassed. "I mean should I go with you to your mother and tell her or not?" "No please don't we promise to do whatever you want too" they said to me. I thought about it for a while and sent her to my room to gain some time. When they were gone, Rosi naturally asked me what that was. The otherwise so bitchy now so subdued.

I told her about my discovery of the two in front of the grandparents' room but not what was in the room. Rosi laughed her heart out. "You have to take advantage of that. You'll never get an opportunity like that again". That was also clear to me, but what should I do with them. Rosi had turned to me in the meantime and was stroking my chest. My morning latte had settled down a bit, but when she crawled further down over my stomach a sizeable tent was set up. Rosi smiled and said, "We don't want to leave him standing around like that. I've got something to take down". She lifted the blanket and disappeared under it. Without further ado, she almost swallowed my penis whole and sucked on it. The blood immediately rose to my head and I tensed up so as not to squirt immediately.

The woman had practice who knows exactly how to do it and she knew it too. Just before I shot down she curbed her activity to start again as soon as I had recovered a bit. I removed the blanket to see what it was doing. We looked at each other and she smiled as best she could with my cock in her mouth.

She licked up at him from below and took off her nightgown. I pulled her to me and a long look turned into the most sensual kiss I've ever received. With a skilful grip, she had my penis firmly enclosed and slowly slipped her pussy over it. My blood boiled in my veins. My pulse was racing and she moved very slowly. My lust grew immeasurably and I began to thrust into her from below.

Her lips parted from mine and a long moan escaped her, initiating her orgasm. By no means too early because I had reached the point a long time ago and I sprayed the largest known load of sperm that I had known up to that point. It felt like hours before our orgasm slowly subsided. She opened her eyes and smiled at me. "I don't usually go that fast," she whispered to me. But now it was time for me to go to the toilet.

A quick kiss and I apologized but quickly left the room. Regardless of the fact that I was still naked and my penis was dripping, I immediately went to the bathroom. The door slammed shut behind me, and then I heard my mother's voice, "Bernd, I'm only here..." Her attention was directed to my piquant spot, which still hadn't swelled up. I instinctively tried to cover up what I was in front of with my hands didn't need to hide from his mother. She had just come out of the shower with only a small towel and was trying to hide with it too. Our efforts were probably a bit childish and we both had hearty laughs.

"What do you want?" she asked. "I have to urgently" was my answer and shook from one leg to the other. "Then do it quickly, I'll look away too." "You don't need that, I think you've seen that happen to me many times before". Her eyes darkened. "You were 10 years younger then," she said a little snippy. I sat down and had to push my cock down quite a bit. Finally a blessing.

My mother had turned around and continued to dry herself. Her figure is impeccable, a rounded pelvis, narrow shoulders and her round breasts are clearly visible past her rib cage. When she bends over her pussy lips come out at the back and damn it I almost peed on myself. But he gets stiff at the sight of my mother. Now get out of here quickly. A kiss to my mother and quickly away. For the first time I curse my grandmother's experience as a child.

When she was a little girl, she locked herself in and couldn't open the door from the inside. Her father had to smash the door with an ax because it made her panic and scream. Since then there have been no keys to lock the doors in my grandma's house. Totally out of breath I came into the room and of course Rosi saw my swinging phallus. "Oh, who fired you up then". I say the woman is great and always honest with me. But my explanations of what I experienced were only half the truth. "Then I'll go to the bathroom now, a good opportunity to be alone with your mother be" my blood rushed to my head, my thoughts were racing.

Rosi had only taken one of her seductive panties and a sweatshirt and disappeared. What did she want with my mother now? I was already concocting all sorts of excuses in my head when there was a knock on the door. It was Sara. "Okay, if you really want to, it'll stay between us for now. If you follow some things. There's no bitching anymore and if you annoy me you can go to your mother yourself. You only speak to me when I ask you to. And a few other things I'm still thinking about."

She gaped at me and nodded vigorously. "Then go to your sister now and follow my instructions. I'll see you at breakfast." She left in a hurry and I really enjoyed commanding her. At breakfast they were very sweet. They kept looking at me and tried to appear normal to the outside world. Katrin noticed her reserve and immediately suspected an illness and felt them on the head to see if they had an elevated temperature.

Grandpa announced that we would start right away to get the Christmas tree. He drove into the forest with the children and always looked for a nice tree that everyone would bring home together. That was almost a tradition and everyone was looking forward to it, because grandpa had usually prepared something else for fun. Rosi and my mother came and were very happy.

Mother looked at me and her eyes narrowed to small slits and she said to me "We're both still talking". I suspected that a lecture would follow and got ready to tighten the sled with Grandpa. My photo case and tripod I had already packed my cousins. "We'll make ourselves comfortable in the back and the little ones can ride in the front with grandpa on the box". Apparently they understood and organized some more blankets. We drove 20 minutes and then grandpa stopped the sled in the middle of the forest.

"We'll see if we can find something suitable here," he said and got off. After a few meters there was a fir tree with lots of sweets and the little ones were of course enthusiastic. They collected everything and quickly ate some away. Grandpa came up to me and watched me taking pictures, he pulled out a hip flask and said "Then let's start the coming festival first" and handed me one too.

That was devil's stuff for lumberjacks or so I said. Grandpa laughed and handed me the saw "Since you mention it. Here this year it's your turn to cut down". We went to the tree and I cut off the lowest branches. The tremor loosened the snow on the branches above and of course it came down right on top of me. Everyone started laughing and I caught started a snowball fight, after I landed a few hits I took some more pictures and then sawed down the tree.

Grandpa and I tied the tree to the back of the sled and we drove towards the farm. My cousins on either side of me. Everyone was pretty wet and cold from the snowball fight. I gave the others another blanket and put my arms around Sarah and Judith. The two were shivering from the cold and I rubbed their shoulders. They actually snuggled up to me and their hands sought a warm spot.

Grandpa looked back at us for a moment and nodded at me with a wink. At first I didn't understand but then I thought why not. I slid my hands on her shoulders forward to the cleavage and felt cozy warmth. Little by little I felt my way forward and her skin felt velvety soft. When I got to their breasts, the two looked at each other and Sarah sighed softly. They moved even closer and her hands made their way under my sweater. I felt her breasts with my fingertips.

Sarah elicited a sigh again and Judith said "Shhh!" I assume so Grandpa doesn't notice anything. I touched her nipples with my index fingers and now Judith couldn't keep still either. Her nipples weren't just stiff because of the cold. I twirled them carefully and the sighs that escaped their lips gave me the certainty that they were horny now.I played with the nipples a little more until we were almost in the yard.

Grandpa brought the tree to the house with the little ones and asked me to unhitch the sled and take care of the horses. No problem, I had done that many times before, but this time the two of them should help me. I untied the horses and had them push the sleigh into the barn. On snow it was relatively easy, but in the barn there was only a simple floor and they had to make quite an effort. They made it and I told them to go into the house and put on something dry first. I led the horses into the stable and unharnessed them. Now I led the first horse into the box and wanted to devote myself to the second when I again heard clear noises from the other end of the stable.

I immediately took my camera and crept to the box. I thought a few more pictures of Gerda with Jakob wouldn't go amiss either. I peeked into the box from a sharp angle and had my camera ready.

As expected, Jakob knelt behind -- that wasn't Gerda. I couldn't see who it was here and went to the other side. With the camera on my eye, I looked at Uncle Klaus's ass.

Jakob just fucked him in the ass. In shock, I triggered the automatic function and it flashed several times in a row. The two jumped up and I got out of the field as fast as I could. In the house, grandma came towards me and said I should come to the kitchen to drink cocoa. That suited me best to hide in the crowd. Aunt Katrin my mother and the little ones were already there and drank the hot cocoa. My mother scowled at me again, as if she knew I'd put my foot in it again.

A short time later Klaus came and sat down next to me. He wanted to start another conversation about the military is good and come and have a look. It burned my fingers to tell everyone what I had not only seen. I looked at him and said "Aunt Katrin?" He was stiff as a stick. "What's the matter with Bernd?". I looked questioningly at Klaus and he shook his head, only visible to me. "Can you deliver a message from me to your husband?" He turned ashen pale in the face. "What?".

"I'm not going into the military. And if he doesn't stop annoying me, I'll write a photo postcard to the Minister of Defence". That did it, he stopped breathing and the others laughed. "If you fight again this year, I'll smash your heads together," said my grandmother . Sarah and Judith also came into the kitchen. They had put on leggings and a matching jumper that must have been from last year because it stretched nicely over the curves. Klaus left and Grandpa came and sat next to me.

He put an arm around my shoulders and hugged me. "How's your A-levels going?" he asked. I told him that everything was fine and that I would certainly pass with a good grade point average. "I'm still looking for a successor for the farm. If you like. The horses you're having fun, aren't you?" He nudged me in the side and blinked at my cousins. “They are only a few months younger than me and will graduate next year. Maybe one of them will take over the farm." I answered. We all really needed the cocoa. Warmed up, I wanted to take a few more pictures and invited the two to pose for a bit. "Yes, take a few photos of the two. We have haven't made one for a long time" said Katrin. So the three of us went to find a suitable place. The two had become really pretty late bloomers just but pretty. They didn't say a word and followed me to the small hill behind the stables. It was a bit difficult here, but there was already almost half a meter of snow and we sank deeply with every step.

The light was very good the sun was clear and high in the sky. I conducted them and took some pictures. The poses they had to hold made them a little warm in their thick jackets and I said "Take them off". They had nothing on under their sweaters and their nipples stiffened immediately. I had already finished one film and the second one was with close-ups. Now I wanted to test how far I could take them. According to their promise, they wanted to do everything I said. "Show me some skin" they looked at me questioningly. "Yes, raise your sweater a bit so that I can photograph your navel". It also got a bit too warm for me and I took off my jacket and laid it in the snow. A few photos later I put both of them on my jacket and asked them if they had kissed before. Both nodded hesitantly. With the sun in the background and her lips touching each other, she made some very nice photographs. My next idea was just the tips of the tongues touching.

They followed everything and did their job really well. "Pick up each other's sweaters a little bit. yes something more And now glide easily over the skin. Some closeups of the goosebumps around the belly button and the nipples pushing through the fabric. "Okay, you're naturals. Show me your breasts," I instructed. Sarah looked at me, but Judith had already pulled her sweater up to her neck. So Sarah immediately took her sweater off completely.

As I thought nothing underneath and her pink nipples stuck out in the midday sun. I've never taken so many pictures at once. "Take some snow and put it on your sister's nipple." Sarah was faster and had a handful of snow and just touched the very tip of Judith's nipple. It seemed to me that it would grow even bigger and escape her mouth a long sigh. Sarah seemed to enjoy this game and drew some lines from left to right breast and navel. The melted snow slowly ran down her skin and collected in the navel. Sarah went in with the tip of her tongue to taste it.

Fantastic pictures that I was now allowed to shoot with wet fingers. Judith pulled up her legs and her slightly too tight leggings stretched in the crotch. Her vulva was clearly outlined and you could see her labia. Sarah saw that too and gently stroked the mound up to the swollen lips. This made everything even more visible and my little friend slowly began to be happy too. The two kissed each other on the stomach when we heard Grandma call.

We were all dressed quickly and went to meet her. She had the food ready and we should come in slowly. A tempting smell came towards us from the kitchen and I wanted to go towards it, but Grandma told me I should get mother and Rosi. I sprinted up the stairs and almost crashed into Klaus, who fled our room while being beaten by Rosi with the rubber cock. "The pig ransacked our things. If your father were still alive, he would beat him up again." Big question mark on my face. Rosi pushed me into the room and said, "I was still very young, but Gerda is a few years older and the house wasn't that big before Boys share a room and I share a room with Gerda.

Because of the screaming, your father came and took Klaus to task." Our room has been completely torn apart. All the drawers are open and things are flying everywhere. I put down my photo bag and then I remember what he was looking for. Of course I have to hide the photos I took well, but where? We cleaned things up and Rosi scolded a few more times and didn't calm down. She then went downstairs and I to Katrin's and mother's room. I knocked softly. Nothing no one seems to be there I opened the door and my mother was lying on the bed and had fallen asleep I took her hand and she slowly woke up She saw me with a smile and also reached out her other hand to me.

She pulled me onto the bed and said "We still have to talk". Immediately I felt warm and cold at the same time. All my sins that I had committed and those that I will commit were in my head and threatened to explode. "Come here leg you to me I'll tell you what I should have done much earlier. I was very young at the time and had a boyfriend who was a few years older than me. Well and how it is when he got you around he moves away and war I didn't see him again. In the sadness I was also pregnant. When I met your father, everything was suddenly different. We loved each other from day one and I confessed to him immediately that I was going to have a child that wasn't his . And because you got on so well with him, I haven't told you until now".

She kissed my forehead and pressed my head to her chest. In the past we often just lay there and talked. "I love you, mom. And my father is my father, nothing will change that. He always has been and always will be" I answered her. "That's also one of the reasons why I've never looked for another man. For fear of hurting you or even driving you away from me". "But you don't have to. You're a young, extremely attractive woman, if you want you've got ten on each finger." I slipped my lips. She caught her breath, "You little charmer. Are you serious?" "Of course you should just get yourself a good calendar or they'll step on each other's toes." We laughed and got up.

My mother put her skirt and blouse back in order and I took the opportunity to hide the film in her closet. She smiled at me and said "we'll do that more often from now on, like a little chat".

That was fine with me because I've always enjoyed it immensely. Everyone at the table was already eating and of course we got a lot of ridicule. Only my cousins kept quiet. At dessert, when I watched them, they lasciviously licked the spoon and looked at me as well. The beasts had taken a liking to our arrangement. But that's not how it should work.

"Grandpa? Sarah and Judith asked me if we can turn on the sauna today. You feel a little dull. Definitely a little cold" the color literally fell out of both of their faces. Until now they had always successfully avoided going to the sauna. "Of course Bernd. You know how everything works and can then heat it up". Now I looked at the two and licked my lips. After the meal I went to the basement to organize everything and turned on the sauna. Grandpa had a little paradise here with everything your heart desires. Sauna solarium small swimming pool. It's not deep, but it's enough to swim a few strokes. In the shower area there were enough towels and also lotion and creams available. temperature was set. I went upstairs satisfied. Our room was darkened and Rosi had already laid down. I quickly took off my things and crawled under the covers. "Are you asleep yet?" I asked. "Uhhmmmm" she answered. I slowly approached her and stroked her arm. Her hair smelled like apple shampoo and I kissed her neck.

My little friend slowly stood up and squeezed between her thighs. When I touched her breast - - "Bernd, what are you doing?" That wasn't Rosi's voice. Mother. Of course I was very familiar with the smell of her hair, but once the little man is standing there is no blood to think about You can't just" at that moment the balcony door opened and Rosi came in. She saw what happened and smiled at us. My mother was up in the meantime and looked heavenly. No wonder her figure and otherwise she is very similar to my aunt.

Rosi said, "I told you, the boy is so far and no longer small." "He should just take a better look at who he -" Rosi took her in his arms and hugged her tightly, "Let Aunt Rosi do it. I'll teach him everything." My mother put on her skirt and left us. "We talked a bit and so as not to crumple her skirt she took it off. Then she got a little chilly and slipped under the covers and fell asleep. I took my jogging suit and went to the balcony to have a smoke. Then I heard the scream and came to you immediately".

She took off her jogging suit and what came out underneath was sensational. Her bra panty set consists of a pair of nothings edged in blue lace and the matching garter belt that holds the blue satin sheers in place. Her black hair is shiny and her skin looks like ivory. I catch my breath as she gets under the covers and kisses me. We caress each other and I'm looking forward to the last. Rosi notices this and turns me onto my back. She sits on me and massages my muscles from my shoulders down.

On the stomach she makes extra slow to torture me even more. My hands run over her body and trace her shape. I circle her bra and brush the straps off her shoulders with my fingertips. As I uncover her breasts, she sighs softly and I begin to feel them with my eyes closed. She sits with her pussy right on my stand and gently slides back and forth a bit. I feel like my testicles are about to burst. She walked a little further forward and I could feel myself slowly entering her. She also had her eyes closed, enjoying the moment. Her panties were open at the crotch so she didn't have to take them off. I tried to thrust into her from below but she pinned me firmly onto the bed.

My lust increased and I wanted to become active, but she wouldn't let me. She slowly began to move up and down and her nipples stood out and I immediately caught them with my lips. Sucking, I let one out of my mouth, smacking it around to catch the other one. She liked that because she held the other one out to me again and again until she came. She almost rolled over and moaned her orgasm in my ear.

Now I had the necessary freedom to act with both hands I pulled her butt up a little and thrust into her from below. I banged like a maniac and she cummed on me again. My testicles spasmed and one beam after the other was sent on its journey. Tightly entwined we stayed and dozed off a bit.

A soft knock on the door startled us. "May I come in?" we heard my mother ask. "Come in" called Rosi and made no attempt to cover herself. "I don't want to disturb you, but I just put on your skirt in a hurry," she said and had already taken it off and took the other one. She was gone just as quickly as she was there.

Rosi and I looked at each other and had to laugh. "On to the second round" she said and with her hands she started to bring my somewhat collapsed back to life. When it wasn't going fast enough for her she turned around and came with her beautiful bottom over my face and put her mouth over mine little friend who awoke joyfully to new deeds.

With slightly trembling fingers I shared her panties with the labia and our juice slowly ran out of her. I stuck out my tongue and tested the liquid which made me even hornier. I licked her cunt the full length and I sucked on the clitoris until she moaned every time. Her mouth closed tightly around my penis and she sucked until my balls boiled. She knew exactly how far she could go before I cummed she stopped again and slowed down to start her game again.

"Put a finger in my back," she whispered. Nothing better than that. My finger stretched her pussy just a little, so all the juice came out. I licked it all up the more I came, the wilder I got " she got louder. I didn't understand right away and she turned around and smiled at me. "You haven't done that yet?" my face gave her the answer because I had no idea what she wanted. "You should do me anal. Some women like it and I love it from time to time".

She led my finger to her cunt to wet it nicely. Then a little deeper and I felt her anus. She pressed my finger lightly against it and he slipped in. A long sigh escaped her and I became a little braver. I put my thumb on her clitoris and squeezed it a bit. Her pelvis circled a little and her breathing quickened, an orgasm announced itself. My thumb found its entrance and for the first time I felt the thin membrane between the entrance and the exit (or vice versa). Her body trembled and she pressed her hands to her breasts. My tongue searched and found her clitoris and Rosi screamed out her orgasm.

Again and again her body reared up and then collapsed to push her pelvis against my hand again. I had never experienced a woman's orgasm so intensely. It was so intense and so long that I thought she would faint at any moment. After a few minutes she calmed down and took me in her arms. "That was good, I needed it. Now let's do it right". What did I do wrong if we do it right now? She knelt down and gave herself a few smacks on the bottom "Come on I want to feel your cock now".

That was an announcement that even I understood. My plump in hand I approached her. She looked over her shoulder at me and grabbed my spear through her legs. She led it to her pussy and pulled the tip a few times through her gorgeous labia. He was also allowed to dive in a bit. "So and now keep still" with these words she had held my erect penis to the bursting point of her back entrance and pressed against it.

From above I saw how first the tip and then the whole glans disappeared into her anus. An immense warmth and closeness welcomed me and cast a spell over me. She let go of him and said, "Now slowly move on". I moved carefully back and forth piece by piece. She had pressed her face into the pillow and her body was trembling again. "Push me. Fuck me really hard". This announcement well you know. I couldn't keep up my pace for long, the new environment excited me enormously and I already felt it rising. I wanted to pull it out but Rosi noticed and yelled "Squirt it in me".

A few final thrusts and I ejaculated like never before. Drenched in sweat and exhausted, I sank onto the bed next to her. She stroked my hair and I have never felt happier in my life. We didn't need to talk about it, we both knew this was the best thing I've ever experienced. It was getting late if I wanted to go to the sauna before dinner I had to hurry. Rosi slept a little and I kissed her neck and licked her ear. I left the room wearing only a bathrobe. Katrin came towards me and said the two would be waiting. That was good, so they followed my instructions.

Without knocking, I opened her door and entered the room. "Well then, let's go down to the sauna." I said and looked at two somewhat anxious faces. "I won't eat you. Not yet". It looked like they were only wearing a bathrobe. I went out and the two followed me. Everything was quiet in the basement, so we were alone. In front of the sauna I grabbed three towels but not the big ones but the middle ones. I hung my bathrobe on the wardrobe and turned around. Sarah and Judith stared at my penis and couldn't move.

"Come on, take off your coat and here are your towels." I threw one at each of them and roused them from their rigidity. They opened their bathrobes and they actually had a bikini underneath the door. A pleasant warmth hit my face and I sat down on the bottom bench. The two came in and tried to cover their nakedness with the towels. They sat down across from me. "They're for sitting on, not for holding." They understood and sat down very quickly, crossing their legs and holding their hands protectively in front of their breasts. The two of them were really a bit backward but cute as they sat there so tightly.

"Relax a little. You can also lie down if you like. Take it easy, nobody will do anything to you that you don't want to do yourself". Apparently they really relaxed. But their eyes kept going between my legs. I spread them extra wide and leaned towards the stove to make an infusion. They almost fell eyes out. I watched her a little and said "I know you've already seen something like that. You saw exactly what grandma was doing there, didn't you?" they nodded vigorously but couldn't get a single word out of their mouths. "But you haven't told me yet."

They looked at each other and neither wanted to start. "Sarah tell me what you saw". "Not much just how

touch it and take a good look at it". Which they both did. Sarah carefully put her hand on my shaft and wrapped her fingers around it. Her eyes lit up and she started massaging him a little.

Judith had concentrated on my tip. With her finger she explored the slowly bulging glans. I stroked their backs. I grabbed a little more courageously at the beginning of the bottom. They got braver and took turns. Now my testicles were also examined in detail. My magnificent specimen stood like one and demanded redemption again. They figured it out quickly and jerked my cock. I was about to walk a little further when we heard voices.

Judith and Sarah quickly changed benches and sat across from me again. Rosi and my mother came in and sat at the head end. They were so engrossed in their conversation that they didn't even notice the two of them staring at them. Rosi talked in detail about her last boyfriend and what a magnificent specimen he had between his legs. It would all have been nice if he wasn't already married. I took the opportunity and laid my head on my mother's lap. My penis jutted straight up and the twins stared open-mouthed.

Mother slowly stroked my hair and continued talking to Rosi. It was Rosi who first noticed my boner and made a comment, "It wasn't quite as beautiful as Bernd's, but it was just as big." My mother was a little confused but then understood and looked closely at my member don't show it like that in front of the girls". "Would you rather I sit down behind her?" Rosi laughed and pointed to the two of them. They were still sitting there with their mouths open and had turned red.

We joked around a bit and I was getting out of breath. We've been in the sauna long enough. I gave my mother a sweaty kiss on the cheek and wanted out. Judith and Sarah jumped up and crowded in front of me. Well, then they deserve it. In the shower area there were two showers and of course they got there before me.

But I quickly took the water hose off the wall and turned it on full. The first thing I caught was Sarah, who immediately stood stock still and couldn't breathe. Judith noticed something and turned around the moment the beam hit her. Full broadside across her torso. After the first shock, of course, there was a big fight about the water hose. The two screamed and splashed themselves more wet than me. Because of the loud screaming, Rosi and my mother came and actually just wanted to see if something had happened.

The hose found two new victims and a five-person water fight is even more fun. After we were all showered with the hose several times, we went over to the pool. I slide gently into the water, Judith and Sarah are already there and try to push me under the water. The water fight continued. I had to swallow some water, but so did the two. We romped around a bit and then rested in the flat. Rosi and my mother swam a few laps and you could see exactly what a fabulous figure they both have by their silhouettes in the water. I lay down on one of the quiet couches and watched the women.

On the one hand, the two still very small and delicate cousins, on the other hand, the two mature and stately equipped women. Each had something for itself and one was more beautiful than the other. I was only annoyed that I didn't have a camera with me. "Wait here I'll be right back" I called while running away. Quickly up the stairs to the room, the camera and down to the basement. Just in time. They wanted to get out of the pool when they saw me.

"Bernd you can't do that, I'm your mother," she was indignant. Rosi was the first and said, "Who should have anything against that, it's just a few pictures," she struck a pose and motioned to the others. Judith came second and stood next to Rosi and imitated her in every movement. Sarah came to the other side and joined. "Now don't be like that, Erika, come here, we'll also stand in front of you," said Rosi and winked at me and the twins. The three stood in front of the stairs and my mother slowly came out of the water. She had reached the last step and jumped the three aside and I was able to take some pictures of my mother running away.

Rosi and the twins laughed their hearts out and ran after my scolding mother. She came to me in her bathrobe, "Don't show anyone the pictures," she threatened with her finger and her bathrobe gaped at the front so I could quickly take a frontal photo. But now I had to see that I could get away. Quickly up the stairs and Come in. Shortly afterwards Rosi came and we lay down on the bed and she held me in her arms.

Somehow I had an irrepressible thirst for action after going to the sauna and thought about what else I could do. Rosi said I could still ride a little. The idea was really good. I dressed accordingly and went straight to my cousins' room. They sat on the bed in their nightshirts and played cards. "Let's get dressed, we'll ride for another round through the forest," I called and left the room in the direction of the stable. Jakob was very helpful and brought me all the things and the horses. We were done with the second horse, and Judith and Sarah came. " But we can't ride well. And we don't have the right clothes either," they said, somewhat embarrassed. "I'll teach you how to ride properly and make it fun too".

I led Sarah to the first horse and she put her foot in the stirrup. I grabbed her butt and lifted her up. Judith was already standing at the second horse and I also grabbed her bottom and pinched a little tighter. As she sat upstairs she looked at me with wide eyes. I saddled myself and slowly left the stable. "We'll take it very slowly and just do a little lap". My grandfather's horses are all very calm and undemanding, not hotspur Horses not faster that would have been too dangerous After about 20 minutes we had crossed the forest and I steered onto an old track to the neighbors.

I often went with my son during the holidays and we made the area unsafe. The yard was clean but nobody was in sight and everything was dark. I strolled around the old barn where the car was actually parked, but everything was empty there too. We started our way back a bit disappointed. Sarah and Judith had kept up very well so far. Back I wanted to ride around the forest and that's how we got onto the road which was very smooth.

Judith's horse slipped and she landed hard in the ditch. The horse was gone and she let out a piercing scream. I was with her immediately and got her out of the depression where there was still water. All her leggings and parts of the jacket and sweater were soaked. Even worse was a foot she had injured (sprained) the shoe was gone and we didn't find it either. I took her on my horse and slowly headed home. She was pretty cold and I opened my jacket and she crawled in as best I could. Grandpa was already waiting in front of the house.

Jakob had already brought the runaway horse into the stable. I handed over my little frostbite and brought the horses into the stable as well. Sarah and Judith had already gone upstairs when I came into the kitchen. Grandma told me that it wasn't so bad, only if Katrin noticed that I could prepare myself for a sermon. I didn't care now, first of all I wanted to see how she was doing. There was no one in the room then they could only be in the bathroom.

In the bathroom, Sarah was just putting on a lotion. Judith was standing in the shower and hadn't noticed that I had come in. The whole room was filled with a sweet scent and moisture settled on all smooth surfaces. Sarah smiled at me and I went over to her and rubbed her back. Over her shoulders to her hips and on to the small mounds with the nipples rising. She had her hands clasped behind her neck and pushed her breasts forward to show them off even more.

"It was great how I rode the horse with Bernd," came the muffled voice from the shower cubicle. I made the movement with my finger on Sarah's lips so that she shouldn't say that I was here. "Why was that so great?" asked Sarah. "Because I could exactly feel his thing on my leg. I would have loved to have it in my hand again, like in the sauna. It's just a pity that Aunt Rosi and Aunt Erika came along". That's how they liked our little game.

I pushed Sarah forward a little and had my hands on her butt and massaged the lotion in gently. "What would you have done if they hadn't come?" asked Sarah. "I would have jerked him off and if he had injected I would put the cream on your face and rub it in, it's supposed to give you a nice complexion. And you what would you have done?".

My little friend was already too tight in his pants. Without further ado, I quickly took off my pants. "I don't know exactly, maybe I would have even put it in my mouth". Now I was impressed. Sarah was pretty horny as I could tell. I sat down on the edge of the bathtub and looked at her vulva carefully. Her labia were thick and the clitoris just peeped out at the upper end.In the gap, the moisture was spreading, which was certainly not just from the shower.

With the palm of my hand I glided over her mons pubis and she spread her legs a little. I stroked her skin along the inner thigh to the back of the knee and up the other leg to just below her lips. She sighed loudly and Judith said "Are you jerking off your pussy again?". "Come too! Otherwise you would have finished showering for a long time" she answered. I stroked her lips with my finger and pressed gently on her clit. "You're right, we'll save that for later." Come out of the cabin. Judith turned off the water and called "Give me a towel." I quickly grabbed one and held it in front of me so she couldn't see me. She opened the door and took a step out and turned around. I wrapped the towel around her body and gently rubbed her shoulders down to her bottom. I grabbed her hips and went to her breasts.

They were a bit smaller but also stronger. The nipples straightened up immediately and she said, "Don't make me so horny or I'll cum." I kissed her neck gently and pulled her to me. It took a few seconds, but then she realized that I wasn't her sister Her breath stopped and she slowly turned her head. With wide eyes she looked at me anxiously and was about to start scolding her sister when I kissed her.

First she wanted to withdraw but then she answered him and wrapped her arms around me. My hands continued to explore her body and found the cute mounds of her butt. I traced the outline and followed the butt crack to her lap. She also had more moisture than would remain when showering. Her small delicate lips ended in a large clitoris that was very sensitive. At my touch on it she let out a moan and her lips parted from mine. I slowly massaged her pussy and she moved her pelvis to my rhythm.

"And what about me?" asked Sarah. "Come here sister, there is always room for you". She came to my left and was hugged by both of us. Judith kissed her on the mouth and grabbed my now fully erect penis with her other hand. "And now you can show me how you wanted to put it in your mouth," she said, holding out the magnificent staff. Hesitantly, she grabbed my shaft and looked at me, hoping that I would say something. You're always big when it comes to chatter, but when the time comes, you give up".

Judith sounded a bit annoyed. "Okay, we'll do it together" said Judith and got on her knees. Sarah followed her immediately and both held my shaft tight. Judith was the braver one, she kissed my tip first. Sarah did the same and

Judith licked it briefly Sarah then did too.My excitement was almost immeasurable I could never have imagined having sex with my two cousins.

Their tongues became more energetic and this time it was Sarah who took my glans completely in her mouth first. Only very gently, but her tongue was not idle. Judith watched the whole thing carefully and when Sarah let him out of her mouth it was her turn. Her lips were already making the typical movements and she sucked on him too. I sighed and asked Judith, startled, "Do you have to inject?" Sarah was now back in the foreground and I lifted Judith to me. I kissed her tongue this time and her arms wrapped around me.

I slowly groped my way to her paradise and she almost ran out. I massaged her clitoris with two fingers and rubbed her cunt from time to time. Sarah was now pleased and sucked him until I could feel her suppository in her throat and she began to choke. But that didn't stop her from trying to get him all the way in her mouth. "You don't have to take it all the way in if you can't," I told her. "But they always do it that way in the pictures," said Judith, blushing.

The two had grabbed their clothes and quickly went into their room my hair in order and then went over to my room. The balcony door is open and Rosi comes towards me in a hurry and embarrassed. "Come on, let's go in" she says and pulls my arm. I'm already turning around when I hear a long sigh followed by a groan.

My curiosity is piqued and I smile at Rosi. "Is that Katrin and Klaus?" "Yes, of course, who else?" I got a little too excited. Rosi isn't usually like that, there's something else. But what. I want to go back to the balcony but Rosi is blocking my way. Without further ado I take her in my arms, lift her up and take her with me. We slowly approach Katrin's window. It is already dark and there is light in the room.

I look inside and see Katrin on all fours licking my mother's pussy. So that's what I wasn't meant to see. But I liked what I got to see. My mother held Katrin's head tightly in both hands and Katrin licked her clit and massaged her pussy with a vibrator. My mother licked her lips and moaned out her orgasm. I just had to photograph it. Quickly took the old camera, although there is a black and white film in it, but it is bright. Rosi wants to stop me but I just smile at her and give her a kiss. In the meantime they have swapped positions and Katrin is now lying on her back. I take some pictures and she lets out a high-pitched scream as she cums.

I want to go back, so Katrin takes a double dildo out of a drawer and says something to my mother, who immediately lies down on the bed and spreads her legs. Katrin lies down opposite her and lets one end disappear into her and the other end into my mother's pussy. Rosi is standing next to me and has pushed her skirt up a bit and her hands will not be idle in her lap. I'm still taking pictures and have to realize that it makes me pretty sharp too. My penis is swollen to bursting again and finally demands redemption. The two have found their rhythm and rock each other to the next climax.

Rosi rolls her eyes and groans softly. It just happened to her too. Only for me he is still unachieved. Mother and Katrin have just finished their game when there is a knock at their door. Sarah is there and tells them to come eat. That's exactly what we're supposed to eat. I push Rosi into the room and close the balcony door. "You won't reveal anything, promise me that" she said to me. My smile on my face spread over my whole body "And if I'll tell you like UNCLE Klaus did with Katrin..." I replied. "You can't do that to your mother. Uncle Klaus is back in the barracks, he's on night duty and won't be back until tomorrow."

"No, no, I'll tell you that you masturbated on the balcony while you were stretching and I caught you."

"You will not. You don't dare." She narrowed her eyes and threatened with her open hand. "Now I'm afraid you're not going to spank me, are you?" we fooled around a bit and then we went to eat. Gerda had also just come from work and was besieged by her three. Grandma hugged me and stroked my hair out of my face "Sit down, it's getting late". Mother and Katrin were the last ones and Mother sat down next to me. She took me in her arms, hugged me and gave me a kiss cheek."Mmmmh you smell good like aphrodisiacs what is that scent?" I asked and she got embarrassed.

Grandma came in with a pot full of hot sausages, tripped over the edge of the table and spilled the contents across the table. Everyone got something. The food items were bathed in sausage water and the sausages rolled over them. Luckily it wasn't quite as hot as I first thought because I had gotten a pretty good gush on my pants. Not only with me, mother Gerda, her three little ones and the twins also got a lot, only Katrin and Rosi not grandpa came in the door and laughed. Grandma was not only embarrassed now she was also angry.

She scolded and got towels for everyone. We ate and joked that Grandma didn't like it at all. After the meal I went straight to our room and took off my wet pants. I went to the bathroom wearing only a t-shirt and underpants to wash my pants a bit. As soon as I had some water in the sink, the door opened and my mother came in. "Good idea, I was about to do that too." She quickly took off her skirt and came to me at the sink. She was wearing black stockings with a garter belt and matching panties. She caught my gaze and grinned at me. "Do you like your mother Not?" "And if I like my mother. Almost too good because you have to be careful not to catch your breath." I answered and gave her a quick kiss on the cheek.

She grabbed my pants and skirt and cleaned them both. I put my arms around her from behind and laid my head on her shoulders and watched her wash. "I just saw you," I said quietly. She stopped and asked, "What did you see?". "I saw you with Aunt Katrin having fun with the vibrator on the bed." "Bernd, you know..." she started to stutter certain needs like everyone else. Besides, Katrin likes it". Oops now it was out. "But I still want to tell you something about it. We've done it many times. Until your father died after that I just didn't feel like it anymore. Klaus and your father were often abroad for weeks and so Katrin and I became closer. Katrin told me about her lesbian inclination and at some point we tried it out together. Your father knew it as well as Klaus, but how do you actually know about Katrin's lesbian inclination?"

Next blunder. "The twins told me that Katrin only has such magazines and gay magazines, but they're more likely to be from Klaus." Again the next faux pas. "Klaus has gay magazines?" "Of course he lets Jakob put his foot in his .." Next blunder. "What's Jakob doing?" "I was in the stable and heard such strange noises and when I found the cause I saw Jakob serving Klaus from behind". Now it was out. My mother looked at me in disbelief through the mirror. "I don't believe that now. And Katrin knows that?" “I have no idea about Jacob. We were silent for a while, then my mother said, "We'd better keep that to ourselves." She handed me my pants and we went to our rooms.

03

24 Dec Decorate the Christmas tree

I woke up and an unmistakable feeling pushed me into the bathroom. That was occupied by Rosi and my mother. That could take a while. I thought about going downstairs to the guest toilet, but I decided to wait. Expecting again, my mother soon came out and grinned at me. Without saying a word, she went to her room. I went to the bathroom and immediately looked around at the toilet and finally relief. "Good morning" I heard Rosi say. "Good morning" my eyes looked for her and guessed her in the shower cubicle.

"Are you still showering or are you done?" I asked. "I'm still shaving." She doesn't shave a beard. Curious, I went to her and looked into the cabin. She had one foot up and shaved her labia. She smiled at me and said, "Can you go on, it always gets a bit complicated when you can't see properly".

"But I've never done anything like that before" she put the razor in my hand and pulled me towards her. "With a lot of feeling and like on your neck". I got on my knees and took a close look at her already bare pussy. Further back there was hair up to her anus which I lathered with foam. I carefully put the razor on and made the first tracks. It was wonderful to see the tender pink flesh emerging from behind the razor. I slowly finished my work and rinsed off the remains with water.

My penis stood with pleasure and swayed as I stood up. "I see you had fun." She turned the water on fully and we showered together. I lathered her back and let my fingers slide into her buttocks again and again to feel my work. Rosi had me from head to toe lathered my feet and massaged the lather on my skin.She turned around and bent down after the sponge that had fallen down.She stretched her butt towards me extra slowly and I didn't hesitate for a second and guided my penis to her pussy.

She remained in the crouched position and I introduced him. She was so wet that I could push through to the stop without having to reposition, which she audibly liked. She supported herself on the wall with both hands and I rammed my thing into her again and again. Rosi came and moaned, her thighs trembling with pleasure. I pressed my member firmly into her and gave her time to experience the orgasm. When she started to jerk her butt, I broke the rigidity and pumped into her what I could. My legs were getting weak and it wouldn't be long before I would cum too. Rosi noticed it and turned around and took my penis in her mouth. She vigorously massaged the shaft and sucked the glans at the same time.

I gasped, I'm coming, I'm coming, but she just kept going and sucked me completely dry. The stars slowly disappeared from my eyes and I noticed movement behind me. I turned around and there was my mother standing with my camera in hand. "It will give nice pictures, but your film is full, you have to put a new one in" she said and grinned. Rosi kissed me and we dried ourselves off.

Mom came back with a new film and I was surprised that she noticed too. "We want you to take our picture. Not some boring photos but a little bit sharper with sex appeal. It's best if we start right here." She gave me the camera and I changed the film. I'm looking forward to the pictures when I develop the films at home. Rosi was still standing in front of the mirror and I started to take pictures. Her wet black ones Hair hung slightly curled over the shoulders and touched the base of the chest.

My mother came over and held Rose's breasts from behind as if checking her weight. The nipples hardened and I took some close-up shots. Rosi really got going and presented her body to me like a professional model. Now it was my mother's turn. Rosi opened her skirt and put it away. It was a breathtaking sight, her firm thighs with the suspenders and the classy stockings. She seemed to like it too because you could clearly see her nipples through the blouse which I immediately captured on film. Rosi opened her blouse and two decent breasts held by a hoist came to light.

My little friend perked up and craned his head. The two women smiled at me and had fun with it. Rosi came up to me and said I should photograph her pussy in large format. I lay down on the floor and she stood over me. Her labia were slightly swollen and gave off a slight shimmer of moisture. With both hands she shared her column and I had full insight and photographed all the details. "Come here, Erika, lick my clit," she said, and my mother touched the clit with the tip of her tongue. My penis was already swollen and started to throb. Mother put a finger in Rose's pussy and continued licking the clit. "So now you." Rosi said to my mother, who addressed me in amazement.

"Only if you want, I'll take a few pictures, otherwise I'll put the camera away," I told her. Still a bit hesitant, she stood up and Rosi sat on my penis. I hadn't expected that and gasped for air. Mother was now standing over me and with her vulva in the direction of Rosi, who immediately tampered with her panties. Mother still held him and said "Should I really do that?". Rosi laughed and said "You'll see it's really good when you look at the pictures afterwards". She thought about it a little longer and I first took a picture of her panties, which clearly showed the dampness of her excitement. Then she took them off and I saw that my mother had shaved her whole pussy and not just a part like Rosi.

I almost fell off when I saw it. Rosi gently stroked the bare mound and mother sighed softly. I could hardly take any pictures so much this sight aroused me. When Rosi stuck her tongue into the column, my mother came and had to hold on to Rosi with her hands. Rosi couldn't help it either. A few seconds later her pelvis twitched on my penis, pulling the juice out of my loins. I could hardly think about taking pictures. With a wide aperture, I just hope that I got my mother's orgasm as sharp on the negative as it was.

Completely exhausted we sat three on the floor as the door opened and Sarah looked in. She saw us and wanted to leave immediately, but Rosi said, "Come in." She looked a little embarrassed and mother went over to her, "You've already seen everything, that doesn't need to be uncomfortable. What did you want?". "Actually, I have to" came a little shyly. "Then do it," my mother replied and put on the panties. "But you're all watching me," she said excitedly. "Well, I and Rosi do it the same way and Bernd has seen it many times," she said. I waved her over and when she was close enough I grabbed the hem of her shirt and said "Feel free to show us your little pussy it's very beautiful".

First she still held the fabric in her hands but then released her grip. I lifted her shirt slightly, revealing her slightly hairy pussy. "You look almost like mine" and Rosi held out her pussy for you to look at. With her mouth open, Sarah took a closer look and a small trickle ran down Rosi's thighs. Then she looked at my penis and got big eyes now she had finally realized what was going on here had happened before. I pulled her a little closer and kissed her clit. "I have to urgently" she said and was already on the toilet. As soon as she sat down, we heard a powerful jet flow into the pool and she became red and even more embarrassed.

My mother had dressed so far and gave Sarah a quick kiss on the cheek and went out. Rosi stood in front of the mirror and did her hair. I also headed to our room to get ready for breakfast. I already had my trousers on when Sarah came and asked Are you all together...?". "What do you mean?" I asked consciously. "You know." "I can't imagine what you mean Sarah?" “Did you and Aunt Rosi do it. Really?" "Yes, of course, and it was great fun." "And your mother?" "She just watched" You let her watch when you do it?" ". "May I also watch?" "Of course, tomorrow morning I'll take a shower again, then you can watch".

"I...I...I thought you were fucking" "Oh yes, that too" now her eyes were shining. "And may I?" "What may you?" I lined up extra. "Oh man, Bernd, you know exactly what I mean, I also want to bang." She put her hand over her mouth and stared at me. "So you want?". I turned her around, slapped her bum and led her to the door. "Wanting is not liking. Tell me when you're ready and we'll talk about it again." She went to her room and I went to breakfast.

Grandma had outdone herself again. Everything we like to eat was on the table. Fresh rolls and bread, sausage, cheese, jam and our own honey, fresh eggs from our own chickens and, of course, milk.

"Bernd you can help me put up the tree right away when I come back from the stable," said grandpa. I nodded with my mouth full and grandpa left. We sat for a while and talked. Sarah and Judith kept looking at me and trying to watch me show that they wanted something. But I skilfully ignored this and sang some Christmas carols with my mother and grandma. The three smaller ones wanted to build a snowman and I had nothing better to do until grandpa comes and agreed to take care of them.

Sarah and Judith also came along and took part in rolling up the balls. I asked Jeremiah to get some things from grandma to give the snowman a face. Sarah and Judith wanted to put the top ball down when they lost their balance. Judith fell backwards into the snow with the ball and was almost completely buried under the ball. She was wriggling her legs in the air and I could hardly get her out of her position with laughter. She had the snow all over her mouth in her nose in her ears and some of it fell down her neckline and now slipped deeper when she got up.

She quickly tried to get her clothes out of her pants to drop the rest but instead it fell into her pants and her breath caught and she got goosebumps. "Now your can is finally going to cool down," Sarah writhing with laughter. In the same second, a snowball flew and hit Sarah in the middle of the face, so she sat down. Judith was with her immediately and stuffed hands of white snow into Sarah's neckline. Now it was time for a snowball fight and Grandpa came running and joined in. Jeremias took a beating as soon as he came around the corner of the house. Now they were after me and I ran and pulled out my little camera, "Please be kind!" I yelled when they caught up with me and threw me on the ground. I took the first picture while I was still falling. We then postponed building the snowman until the afternoon. Grandpa gave me to understand that we should talk alone. We went into the stables and looked at the animals.

"Think it over Bernd, I've talked to Grandma and if you want, we'll sign over the farm for you. You've finished school now and can study agriculture or something similar if you want. You know the business with the horses and also with the cattle, it's going well and we want to know that it's in good hands. I can run it for a few more years until you're ready to take it over completely. Grandma and I have already found a new job, we're going to open a club with the neighbors as silent partners or something like that. We've already asked your mother if she wants to be a manager and she wasn't averse but wanted to talk to you about it first. You already know the mares very well.

I was a bit taken by surprise and how did Grandpa know about Judith and Sarah. It would be conceivable that I would let myself get involved. "That's a great offer but also a lot of responsibility, I have to think about it calmly." "We'd wrap that up nicely for you as a Christmas present," Grandpa joked and punched me on the arm. We strolled arm in arm to the house like two old buddies and grandma already shouted "You two good-for-nothings only have fun on their minds and the tree isn't even in the living room yet". As always, she was right, we should hurry up because it was getting late. Grandpa got tools and I got the Christmas tree stand. We quickly cut off a few lower branches. Made the trunk a bit slimmer to fit and attach to the stand.

Satisfied with our work, we heaved the tree into the hallway. Cursing and crying, Sarah came towards us with a huge basket of laundry. When I asked what's going on, she howled even louder and quickly went into the utility room. Grandpa and I looked at each other questioningly. We put the tree in the corner by the window and grandpa examined the stand. "Then we want to put one on it quickly so that it stands securely," he winked at me ambiguously. Again this homemade one. Just thinking about it gave me a headache.

neck and my second hand found her nipple a tremor ran through her body as her orgasm came. She slowly recovered and we kissed. "That was nice, that's exactly what I needed" she smiled at me.

"Come on, the others are looking for us." We went into the living room and grandpa had another round on the table and handed out the glasses. Sarah was supposed to get one too, but she waved her hand vigorously and said, "No, if mom sees that, I'll get it only more trouble" and ran upstairs. "I think we have to talk to Katrin sometime, it can't go on like this, the girls are old enough, she should give us some freedom," Grandpa said and cheered us.

"Bernd, why don't you take a few pictures?" Grandma called. I heard the vacuum cleaner halfway up the stairs. Judith was cleaning my room. She pulled at the hose and mobbed to herself. I walked behind her and covered her eyes as well She wanted to free herself but when I kissed her on the neck she calmed down. Her movements were like in slow motion. I caressed her neck and my hands caressed her body. The nipples were excited under the sweater and she always twitched a little when touched She turned her head so we could kiss, pressing her butt onto my already swollen genitals.

She was wearing jogging pants and I was looking for the clasp. A small loop prevented the pants from slipping. A small train at the right end and you had a clear path to the most beautiful place in the world. Her bare skin was silky soft and warm. You can hardly feel the fluff on her mound and her labia are already wet. She sighed when I touched her. My index finger parted her crack and her little clit was extremely sensitive. Her pelvis jerked uncontrollably and she came instantly. She almost screamed but I closed her mouth with mine.

Without saying anything else, I picked up the camera and headed back downstairs. Everyone was busy hanging balls and candles on the tree. Mother had put on the garlands and was dancing to the music. Grandpa followed his favorite pastime of giving people so much of his homemade food that they could no longer stand. Grandma struggled with the lighting. If she got a knot out of one end, she'd tied a new one at the other end. Katrin and my mother hung in the tree and tried to distribute the balls evenly. Rosi gave directions and grandpa observed everyone from a safe distance.

However, like every year, the tree was finished and everyone commented on how beautiful it is again this year. "Only this time you forgot the tip" Grandpa laughed. Grandma didn't think it was funny at all and scolded him.

"Bernd get a ladder then we can put the tip on," Grandma pushed me. When I came up with the ladder, there was a loud discussion going on about who should put the top on. Grandpa could hardly contain his laughter and Grandma became all the more angry. In the end, Rosi was given the task.

"Bernd you hold the ladder so I don't fall into the tree," said Rosi. Step by step she climbed the ladder all the way to the top. She still had to stretch to get to it and lifted one leg. From here below I now had a wonderful view of her bare labia She caught my gaze and said "Oh wait that's all crooked" and repeated the whole thing again. "Did you like what you saw?" she asked as she climbed down. And did I like that. "Now we have to change clothes, otherwise we'll be late for church," cried Grandma.

Don't go to church, it's always so boring, I thought when my mother gave me a kiss on the cheek and said, "Come on, this class won't kill you." I liked that and I agreed. We all went to our rooms and got ready for church. Mother had given me a suit that I wanted to ignore at first but then decided to put it on. Rosi had put on one of her designer dresses and, as almost always, wore suspenders and stockings in the right shade. This time she also wore panties.

I went to the stable and Grandpa and Jakob had already hitched the horses to the sleigh. Jacob said, "See you soon in church." "Is Jacob coming to church too?" I asked in surprise because I couldn't remember that he had ever gone along. "Yes, Jakob has a girlfriend and she goes to church from time to time and of course he goes with him." We drove to the front of the house and I went to the door to get Grandma.

"You and Grandpa will take the children with you and we women will drive the car," she said. All right, the three little ones sat right next to Grandpa on the coach box. Then Judith came, she had a blue, knee-length velvet dress and I helped her get her coat to put on. I accompanied her to the sled and she sat down. Sarah had the same dress on only in dark red, I helped her too and sat down between the two. Grandpa winked at me and cracked the whip. It was good up to church 40 min drive.

I spread out a blanket and handed it to the front. Another wrapped me and the twins in cozy warmth. The two had linked arms with me and put their heads on my shoulder. I put my hands on her knees. The tights were classy and soft. The meat underneath is tender and hot. My fingers slowly slid up her inner thighs. They sat down so that I could continue unhindered. I then felt bare flesh on the upper end of her thighs, she wore stockings and no pantyhose. "If Mama finds out about it, there will be thunderstorms again," I said quietly. "We got them from your mother and Aunt Rosi, they also wear something like that," they replied. I could have driven much longer with two such beautiful women by my side, but we were already there.

We fastened the horses and two more sleighs were there. I went to Judith and Sarah together we walked the short way around the church to the entrance. Grandma Gerda Katrin, mother Rosi and Klaus were already there and waved to us. Gerda was still working and drove straight here. Klaus had caught the women at home when he came back from the barracks. We went in together and found two benches that were free. Mother went to the opposite bench and spoke to a woman.

I couldn't believe my eyes, Mrs. H. and Andrea were sitting there. When Andrea saw me she smiled over at me. Our eye contact went unnoticed by everyone. Then Jakob came in a suit too. I had never seen him like this and wasn't just staring at him because of that. He sat down next to Ms. H. and greeted her with a quick kiss. The sermon was boring as always and just didn't want to end. I thought about how to make something like this more interesting, but I didn't come up with a good idea. I always thought of things that had nothing to do with the church.

Finally the blessing came and the end was near. Now I had another idea. Judith and Sarah didn't know that I already knew Andrea, so I said to them, "If we go out right away, we absolutely have to follow the girl" and looked over at Andrea. The two didn't seem too happy that I was interested in them But we agreed. We got up and Sarah immediately pushed out to come behind Andrea. Judith and I followed her. In the middle of the aisle where the crowd was the heaviest, I whispered to the two of them, "Grab her butt". They looked at me in disbelief. "Come on now". We went a little closer and the two hesitated a bit more but did as they were told.

Andrea twitched briefly looked at me and smiled and looked ahead again. She probably thought I had touched her butt. "Let's go again". And again they made it a little longer this time. I could see Andrea stretching out her buttocks and taking it Church we talked to different people we knew and wished everyone a Merry Christmas and made our way home.

In the sledge Judith asked me "How did you know that she put up with that?". "You can see that when a mare is in heat" I answered. Grandpa and I got the horses ready in the yard and put the sled in the stable. When we got into the kitchen, it smelled like hearty food and everyone was in a good mood. The twins came too and now I got my first real glimpse of them. The clothes were guaranteed to be from Rosi's boutique because Katrin would never have bought them such provocative things. The sight of her made me smile when Grandpa noticed and came to me.

"Well, my boy, the mares are due the way I see it," he said quietly. And how right he was, just like every time something came up ?". He laughed "You just have to know that a stallion can make many mares happy, but the mare can also be mounted by another stallion".

How right he was. Grandma called us to dinner and Grandpa patted me on the shoulder. The food was wonderful and we all ate too much, which was another reason for grandpa to give everyone a homemade one. This time Judith and Sarah also got a glass and Katrin and Klaus said "But not just that one anymore". Grandma had probably talked to them and the two were happy about it. But they didn't like it as you could see from their faces but now there are presents" exclaimed grandma and everyone stormed into the living room. The three smaller ones had the most presents and didn't make any progress with unwrapping them.

I was taking the obligatory Christmas pictures when my mother came over with a present. Actually, we had agreed that we wouldn't give each other gifts anymore, but would go out for a nice meal together or something. But I had already thought of something like that and was prepared. I had taken a life-size portrait of her and attached a necklace with a gold-set stone pendant in front of it. We exchanged our presents and I quickly unwrapped mine.

I hadn't expected a telephoto lens that I had wanted for a long time because it was quite expensive and my mother's pension wasn't exactly very high. I was so happy and hugged her and hugged her tightly to me. Grandpa came to us and asked "Have you already thought about it?" We said no, but promised to do it and then let them know. After a few rounds of homemade food, my mother said to me "Let's go for a walk".

She told me about the offer to work as managing director and that she would really like to do it. Because if I'm done with school now and go to university, I would only come home on the weekends and she would be sitting there bored all the time. I was happy for her and encouraged her because it didn't make a big difference to me whether

I was studying here or there. I just wasn't sure if I should start breeding or not.

We passed the stables and clearly heard ambiguous noises. Mom smiled at me and I pointed my finger at her to be quiet. "That must be Gerda again" I said and pulled my mother behind me into the stable. As I suspected, the lutes came from behind out of the last box picture immediately at first sight. It was Katrin with Klaus. He was kneeling behind her and had his cock in her ass. Katrin was lying bent over far down with her face in the straw and moaning wildly. We switched positions and now I had a better view at the two of them. I took picture after picture and mother licked her lips. Klaus had to come at any moment, he increased his speed and Katrin screamed her orgasm into the straw. Klaus pulled his penis out of her anus which was wide open and squirted his load over her back and buttocks. Now my film was full and we crept to the house.

"Have you seen Katrin and Klaus?" Grandma asked. My mother blushed but said "No, why?" "Oh, Klaus has to go back to the barracks and won't come home until New Year's Eve.

When Katrin came in, I couldn't help but make a small comment. "Katrin, what's that in your hair?" She became very embarrassed and searched her hair with both hands. "It looks like straw. You should be more careful when you lie down in the hay." My words did not fail to have their effect. She turned pale as a sheet. "Don't worry I won't tell anyone" I whispered to her.

“I invited Ms. H. and her daughter to coffee with Jakob. I hope that was okay with you?" my mother asked. "That was a good idea, so we can get to know her too" called grandma from the kitchen. Grandpa came with a new bottle and everyone had to try whether he succeeded. After we had also emptied a second bottle I was so full that I had to go to bed.

www.ingramcontent.com/pod-product-compliance
Lightning Source LLC
LaVergne TN
LVHW040909150826
845672LV00007B/1956

* 9 7 9 8 8 4 4 3 8 5 0 8 7 *